by J.E. Bright

HEROES
OF THE
HIGH SEAS

illustrated by
Art Baltazar

raintree

a Capstone company — publishers for children

CONTENTS

ATLANTIS HIGH COMMAND
SEA COMPUTER

STORM

ultra smart

mind communication

underwater breathing

aqua belt

horsepower

AQUAMAN

Species: Giant Seahorse

Place of birth: Atlantis

Age: unknown

Favourite foods: prawns and seaweed

Bio: When Aquaman needs a lift, he calls his superpowered seahorse. With the Sea King on his back, Storm can sail beneath the ocean or ride over the waves at super-speed. He is a pretty good dancer, too!

Chapter 1

WILD WHIRLPOOL

Topo the octopus loved playing music for his friend, Aquaman, the king of the underwater city of Atlantis.

Today, Topo entertained the royal court with a lively tune. He played the drums, the trumpet, and the banjo with his eight tentacles.

Aquaman smiled. He nodded his head to the music. Topo was glad he could make the Sea King forget his royal troubles for a while.

BARK! BARK!

Suddenly, Topo's concert was interrupted. A seal named **Ark** rushed into the throne room.

"My king!" Ark shouted. "Red alert! **The city is in terrible danger!**"

"Explain," Aquaman commanded.

Ark quickly swam to the throne.

"A giant whirlpool has erupted in the Triton Trench," shouted the seal. "It's growing bigger every minute!"

Topo shivered with worry. The Triton Trench was located far below the city of Atlantis. Few had ever visited the trench's dark depths.

"I can't have my city destroyed," Aquaman said. "We must investigate!"

The Sea King focused hard. In moments, a seahorse named **Storm** burst into the throne room. He had answered Aquaman's silent command.

"Hop on, sire!" Storm trumpeted.

The seahorse was more than twice the size of Aquaman. He was one of the fastest steeds in the underwater world.

Aquaman leapt on to his back.

"Ark, Topo, follow me!" he ordered.

Ark sped after Aquaman. Topo quickly grabbed his violin and bow. The instrument could play beautiful music. It could also be used as a weapon. Then Topo followed his master to the palace exit.

Once outside, Aquaman led his pets along the city streets. People cheered as they saw the Sea King race past. The fish and folk of the undersea city were used to seeing their king hurry away on heroic missions. Still, Topo felt thrilled by their roar of praise.

Topo could not swim as fast as Ark or Storm. He grabbed on to the seahorse's tail. He held tight as Storm carried Aquaman into the wild ocean outside Atlantis. **WOOOOSH!**

Right away, Topo spotted the funnel. It swirled out of the Triton Trench. The funnel grew wider as it churned up to the ocean surface. **It looked like a giant underwater tornado.**

Topo the octopus held on tightly. Storm the seahorse charged towards the spinning vortex.

Storm stopped at the edge of the trench. Up close, Topo saw that the whirlpool was getting larger. It was growing with bursts of power.

Topo let go of Storm and looked into the trench. He could feel the strength of the whirlpool pulling at him. He clung to rocks with his tentacles.

The vortex swirled downwards. It disappeared into the depths of the trench. The dirty water hid any clue to the funnel's source.

"If the whirlpool gets much larger, it will destroy the city!" said Aquaman.

"Sire, look!" Ark called. He pointed a flipper at the surface. A giant creature was struggling against the powerful funnel.

A female blue whale had been caught in the swirling water. She was trying with all her might not to be sucked down into the trench.

"**Gasp!**" The octopus saw that the blue whale was not alone. She was swimming against the vortex, trying to keep her young calf safe.

MOOANNNN!

The blue whale let out a sad cry. She and her calf began to slip deeper into the vortex. They were losing their battle against the whirlpool.

Aquaman leapt off Storm. He swam over to the whale and her baby.

"I'll help them," the Sea King called to his Super-Pets. "You three go down the trench. **Find out what's causing the vortex, and stop it!"**

Chapter 2

INTO THE DEEP

The Super-Pets dived into the deep, dark trench. Topo rode on Storm's back. Ark swam alongside. They all kept close to the rock wall so the vortex would not suck them in.

As they went deeper into the trench, the vortex got bigger and bigger.

Topo was worried that they would not reach the bottom before the funnel filled the trench. It would rip apart the cliff that held Atlantis.

"**Faster!**" Topo told Storm.

"**Hold your seahorses!** I'm swimming as fast as I can," Storm replied. The seahorse kicked his tail hard. He quickly reached full speed.

The bottom of the trench was still far away. The funnel disappeared into the muddy water below.

A glowing jellyfish swirled past inside the vortex. It spiralled down the funnel faster than Storm was swimming. The jellyfish wriggled in fear.

"Maybe we should ride the vortex," Topo suggested. **"We have to get down there now!"**

Ark the seal smacked his flippers together. **"Let's do it!"** he barked.

"Giddy-up!" Storm shouted. He darted towards the bubbling funnel.

Topo clung to the seahorse as the vortex snatched them into its wild swirl. Storm spiralled out of control. He turned upside down, then flipped over again and again.

The vortex tumbled the Super-Pets along its spinning chute. Ark suddenly shot past the seahorse. He was pulled down the watery tornado.

Topo reached out a tentacle. He wrapped it around Ark's tail. **They needed to stick together.**

"**Keep swimming!**" Topo yelled at Storm. "We won't be tossed around so much if you swim along the swirl!"

The seahorse gave his tail a quick thrust. **THWAP!** With Storm wriggling his powerful body, the pets rode the whipping water downwards.

Topo peered out at the sides of the trench swirling past. Up ahead, near the sandy bottom, the vortex suddenly arched sideways. "Push out!" Topo screamed. "Don't follow the funnel! **Dive to the sand!**"

Storm pushed through the funnel's wall. At the curve where the vortex turned, the pets jumped free.

They smacked down on the ocean floor. **THUD!** Topo's head was spinning. He had managed to hold on to Ark's tail during the ride.

"Talk about sea sickness!" Topo said with a laugh. **"My head is swimming."**

Through his dizziness, Topo saw that the vortex was coming out of a lava tunnel. The tunnel was located in the side of the trench. The volcano that had created the mountain under Atlantis was long extinct. Still, the rock was dotted with old lava tunnels.

Something inside the tunnels was causing the vortex. Topo led Storm and Ark over to it to take a closer look.

The Super-Pets followed the tunnel until they reached a cave. Topo spotted a light glowing ahead. Then he heard a strange grinding sound.

"What is that?" the octopus asked. He swam closer to the light.

The light was coming from a strange sea creature. The animal looked like a fat grub. It had a glowing spot on its forehead.

"It's a diggler!" Topo shouted.

Topo had never seen a diggler up close. They were rare and usually spent their lives tunnelling through the ocean floor, looking for food. They were known to be gentle and harmless. But this one seemed ready to attack.

"Why is it tunnelling into the mountain?" Ark asked. "Is it lost?"

"I don't know," Topo replied. **But then he saw why the diggler was acting so strangely.**

By the light of the diggler's glowing spot, Topo could see **two large manta rays** poking the poor creature. They dived down at it, snapping their tails. The diggler let out a squeal.

"I know those mantas," Topo said.

"Me, too," Ark whispered. *"Misty and Sneezers!"*

"Black Manta's pets," Topo added quietly. "Up to no good."

Black Manta was Aquaman's worst enemy. He had often tried to steal the ocean's treasures or destroy Atlantis.

Topo sneaked closer to watch Misty and Sneezers bully the diggler. They made the creature dig more. When the diggler broke through the rock, water rushed into the empty lava tubes.

SPLOOOOOOSH!

As water flowed into these tubes, it began to swirl like a flushing toilet. This was causing the vortex!

"Just a few more tubes," Misty growled. "Then the vortex will cause the whole cliff to crumble, taking Atlantis with it!" She laughed nastily.

"Uh ... Yeah!" Sneezers agreed.

"No," Topo said firmly. **"That's not going to happen."**

Chapter 3

SOUNDS OF VICTORY

Misty and Sneezers whirled around.

Their eyes widened when they saw the

Super-Pets standing in front of them.

"If it isn't Aquaman's little pets,"

Misty sneered.

"Yeah," Sneezers added.

"We're bigger than you!" Ark said.

"The only size that matters," Misty replied, "is the size of the vortex!"

She spanked the diggler on the rump. The tunnelling creature sped over to the next tunnel in the rock. "This last tunnel will make the vortex big enough to destroy Atlantis!"

"Stop the mantas!" Topo told his friends. **"I'll stop the diggler!"**

Ark and Storm rushed at the evil manta rays. Ark spun around and whapped Sneezers with his tail.

Storm did the same to Misty and sent her spiralling away. The mantas soared back, trying to bite.

While his friends were busy with the battle, Topo tried to work out how to stop the diggler.

Usually digglers were peaceful. The mantas had made this one angry and out of control. If only Topo could calm the diggler's anger.

"Music soothes the savage beast," Topo whispered. The octopus whipped out his violin and started to play.

Topo kept the music slow and tried to relax the diggler. At first, it did not seem to be working. But as Ark and Storm forced Misty and Sneezers further away from the diggler, the music began to have a soothing effect.

The diggler slowed his tunnelling. His body relaxed. He turned to look at Topo with his tiny eyes.

The diggler still had his teeth showing. They were sharp enough to bite through solid rock. **The octopus played a long note on the violin.**

Finally the diggler's mouth closed. With no new tunnels opening up, the vortex's churning slowed.

"Good boy," Topo whispered. "Nobody will hurt you anymore."

Seeing what Topo had done, Misty and Sneezers tried to push past Storm and Ark to reach the diggler.

"I wouldn't," Topo said softly. **"I know polka music as well."**

"Yikes! Let's get out of here!" Misty yelped.

"Yeah!" Sneezer added. He and Misty slipped away down the tunnel.

"Follow them," Topo said. "They're probably going to wherever Black Manta is hiding!"

The octopus leapt on to Storm's back. They zoomed after the escaping manta rays. Topo noticed that the diggler was following, too.

Misty and Sneezer rushed along the bottom of the trench. Topo, Storm, and Ark followed closely behind.

Then suddenly the mantas ducked behind a large, oval rock.

"We've got them cornered!" Ark cheered.

"Wait!" Topo said. **"I don't think that's a rock."**

A row of lights along the oval object flashed on, momentarily blinding everyone. **It was Black Manta's submarine!** On top of the submarine, a hatch slid open, and Black Manta's helmeted head rose out of the opening.

"Look what we have here," the villain said in his deep voice. "So you had my pets on the run, did you? **Let's see if you can handle *me*!**"

Sneezers peeked out over the top of the submarine. **"Yeah!"** he added.

Topo clung to Storm's back. He did not doubt his friends' strength, but he knew just how dangerous Black Manta could be. Even Aquaman had struggled to defeat the villain in the past. Topo was not sure if they could win a battle with Black Manta.

Topo was
determined to do
his best to stop
the villain from
escaping.

Then an
incredibly loud, high-pitched whine
filled the trench from behind Black
Manta.

Black Manta whirled around.

The fiend came face-to-face with one
angry female blue whale. The whale
completely dwarfed the villain.

Aquaman swam beside the blue whale. "Your vortex made this mother whale quite unhappy," Aquaman called to Black Manta. "Maybe you should have thought twice before endangering her child."

"Eep!" Black Manta squealed. He ducked back into his submarine. His mantas followed. The submarine took off, zooming upwards.

"Go ahead," Aquaman told the blue whale. "I'll keep an eye on your young one."

The blue whale grinned and then shot up, too. She chased the submarine out of sight. Topo had no doubt that the blue whale would chase Black Manta across the entire ocean.

"Congrats on stopping Black Manta!" Aquaman told his friends. **"What was causing the vortex?"**

Topo pointed a tentacle at the diggler. **"The mantas angered this tunneller,"** the octopus said. "He didn't mean to cause trouble. Misty and Sneezers were driving him crazy."

"A diggler!" Aquaman said delightedly, swimming over to the grub-like creature. "I haven't seen one of those in years." He patted the diggler on the back. "How did you calm him down?"

Topo pulled out his drums. "Like this," he said, and the octopus began to play a bouncy tune that echoed along the walls of the Triton Trench.

The baby blue whale sang along. It swam in circles and danced. His mother returned and joined in.

Aquaman, Storm, and Ark all joined the calf's dance as well. After a moment, the diggler wriggled in a happy jig, too.

Topo smiled. Thanks to his friends, both old and new, Atlantis was safe once again.

THE END

Krypto

Streaky

Beppo

Comet

Ace

Jumpa

Whatzit

B'dg

Storm

Topo

Ark

Hoppy

Paw Pooch

Bull Dog

Chameleon Collie

Hot Dog

These are **HERO PETS.**

Tail Terrier

Tusky Husky

SUPER-PETS

Ignatius

Chauncey

Crackers

Giggles

Artie Puffin

Griff

Waddles

Rozz

Dex-Starr

Glomulus

Misty

Sneezers

Whoosh

Pronto

Snorrt

Rolf

Squealer

Kajunn

These are **VILLAIN PETS.**

JOKES

What do you call an outlaw octopus?

What?

Billy the squid!

What kind of horse swims under water?

Beats me.

A seahorse, of course!

What happens when you throw a blue rock into the Red Sea?

I dunno.

It sinks, silly!

GLOSSARY

extinct volcano that has stopped erupting

polka fast dance in which couples swirl around the floor in a circle pattern

tentacle long, flexible limb used by an octopus for moving, feeling, and grabbing

throne large chair for a king or queen

trench long, narrow ditch

vortex swirling body of water that looks like an underwater tornado

MEET THE AUTHOR

J.E. Bright

J.E. Bright has written more than 50 novels, novelizations, and non-fiction books for children and young adults. He is a full-time freelance writer, and lives in a tiny flat with his good, fat cat, Gladys, and his evil cat, Mabel, who is getting fatter.

MEET THE ILLUSTRATOR

Eisner Award-winner Art Baltazar

Art Baltazar defines cartoons and comics not only as a style of art, but as a way of life. Art is the creative force behind *The New York Times* best-selling, Eisner Award-winning, DC Comics series Tiny Titans and the co-writer for *Billy Batson and the Magic of SHAZAM!* Art draws comics and never has to leave the house. He lives with his lovely wife, Rose, big boy Sonny, little boy Gordon, and little girl Audrey.

Art Baltazar says:

Read all the DC SUPER-PETS stories today!

Raintree is an imprint of Capstone Global Library Limited, a company incorporated in England and Wales having its registered office at 264 Banbury Road, Oxford, OX2 7DY – Registered company number: 6695582

www.raintree.co.uk
myorders@raintree.co.uk

First published by Picture Window Books in 2011
First published in the United Kingdom in 2012
The moral rights of the proprietor have been asserted.

Art Director and Designer: Bob Lentz
Editors: Donald Lemke and Vaarunika Dharmapala
Production Specialist: Michelle Biedscheid
Creative Director: Heather Kindseth
Editorial Director: Michael Dahl

ISBN 978 1 4747 6441 4 (paperback)
21 20 19 18 17
10 9 8 7 6 5 4 3 2 1

British Library Cataloguing in Publication Data
A full catalogue record for this book is available from the British Library.

Printed and bound in India